Guess what I Have!

ROTHERHAM LIBRARY & INFORMATION SERVICE

10/9/20

This book must be returned by the date specified at the time of issue as the DATE DUE FOR RETURN.
The loan may be extended (personally, by post, telephone or online) for a further period if the book is not required by another reader, by quoting the above number / author / title.

Enquiries: 01709 336774
www.rotherham.gov.uk/libraries

(It rhymes with cook)

First published in 2001 by
Treehouse Children's Books Ltd.,
Shepton Mallet, Somerset BA4 5QE
Copyright © 2001 Treehouse Children's Books Ltd.
All rights reserved.
Illustrations © 2001 Ana Martín-Larrañaga.
Manufactured in China.

CF	
B53 106 487 0	
	13/02/2018
GIFT	£3.99

Guess What I Have!

A flip-the-flap rhyme book

Richard Powell
Ana Martín-Larrañaga

Guess
what I
am
hiding!

(It rhymes with cat)

Guess

what I

am

hiding!

(It rhymes with coat)

It's a boo

It's a **car** !

Guess what I am hiding!

(It rhymes with **icicle**)

bicycle!

Guess

what I am

hiding!

(It rhymes with

baboon!)

It's a
balloon!

Guess
what
I
am
hiding!

(It rhymes with Lulu!)

Guess what I am hiding!

(It rhymes with cook)

But I can't read it.
Can you?

Other Treehouse Flap Books

Guess What I Have!	Powell/Larrañaga
The Happy Cat	Powell/Larrañaga
Tu-Whit! Tu-Whoo!	Powell/Larrañaga
In The Ocean	Powell/Cox
In The Jungle	Powell/Cox
In The Garden	Powell/Cox
On The Farm	Powell/Cox